Elvin and Braveheart Friends Forever

Sandra Morrison

To Mia, my true childhood friend.
She has always been there to share everything
with me, from snacks to problems.
Thank you!

- Sandra M.

Copyright 2022 by Sandra Morrison – All rights reserved.
All rights Reserved.
No part of this publication or the information in it may be quoted from or reproduced in any form by means such as printing, scanning, photocopying, or otherwise without prior written permission of the copyright holder.
Disclaimer and Terms of Use:
The effort has been made to ensure that the information in this book is accurate and complete. However, the author and the publisher do not warrant the accuracy of the information, text, and graphics contained within the book due to the rapidly changing nature of science, research, known and unknown facts, and the Internet.
The Author and the publisher do not hold any responsibility for errors, omissions, or contrary interpretation of the subject matter herein.
This book is presented solely for motivational and informational purposes only.

This book belongs to

_____

Small Elvin was plain, so honest and sweet,
the friendliest mouse you will ever meet.
He lived with Connor, a very kind boy.
His life was full of happiness and joy.

With a lovely home and lots of care,
he did not know these things were rare.
This tiny white mouse with a flattened snout
still dreamed of exploring and going out.

One day small Elvin was home alone
and wanted to take a stroll on his own.
This mouse so small did sniff around.
He climbed the chair, then back to the ground.

He entered the bathroom — what a surprise!
Small Elvin could not believe his eyes.
The tiny mouse climbed up to the shelf.
And in the mirror, Elvin saw himself!

"So, this is me," he scanned his face.
He soon was gone and left no trace!
Oh no! Poor Elvin, all white and plain,
he slipped and fell into the drain!

Oh, that poor mouse rolled left then right.
He was so scared and had no light.
"It is so cold and wet down here!"
Small Elvin cried and shook with fear.

Then Elvin saw two eyes so dark.
"A monster? Ghost? Perhaps a shark?"
It was a cockroach Elvin met.
That bug, it seemed, was not a threat.

Too scared to see, he moved his paws
and ran to flee the monster's claws.
As Elvin tried to wiggle out,
the mouse saw an elongated snout.

Small Elvin felt happy with so much joy.
"A mouse! A girl? Maybe a boy?"
He finally met someone of his kind
with just this question on his mind.

smelly
thin
gray
suspicious
dried cheese
hungry
bubble gum
dirty
unhappy

He asked, "Will you please be my friend?"
The answer he heard was rude in the end.
A mouse, it was Brayden, so thin and gray,
unhappy to meet anyone on the way.

"A friend," he said, "I can't believe!
Oh, you, house mouse, are so naïve.
There's no such thing as friends.
Who claims to be one just pretends."

Small Elvin's eyes were full of tears
as he could not believe his ears,
with thoughts of home and his sweet boy,
and lovely days of happy joy.

"That is not true! My Connor loves me!
Yes, there are friends — you're blind to see!"
small Elvin said and tried to defend
his own sweet boy, his one true friend.

"Then, why did you appear today?
I know your friend threw you away!
It happened to me so long ago.
I had a friend who let me go."

"I was so foolish," poor Elvin cried.
"The grass seemed greener on the other side.
I wanted to see the world and go out.
Was silly of me and my curious snout!"

"I'll help you home," then Brayden agreed.
"But only if you will meet my need.
A meal and a bath are what I ask.
It is not much for such a task."

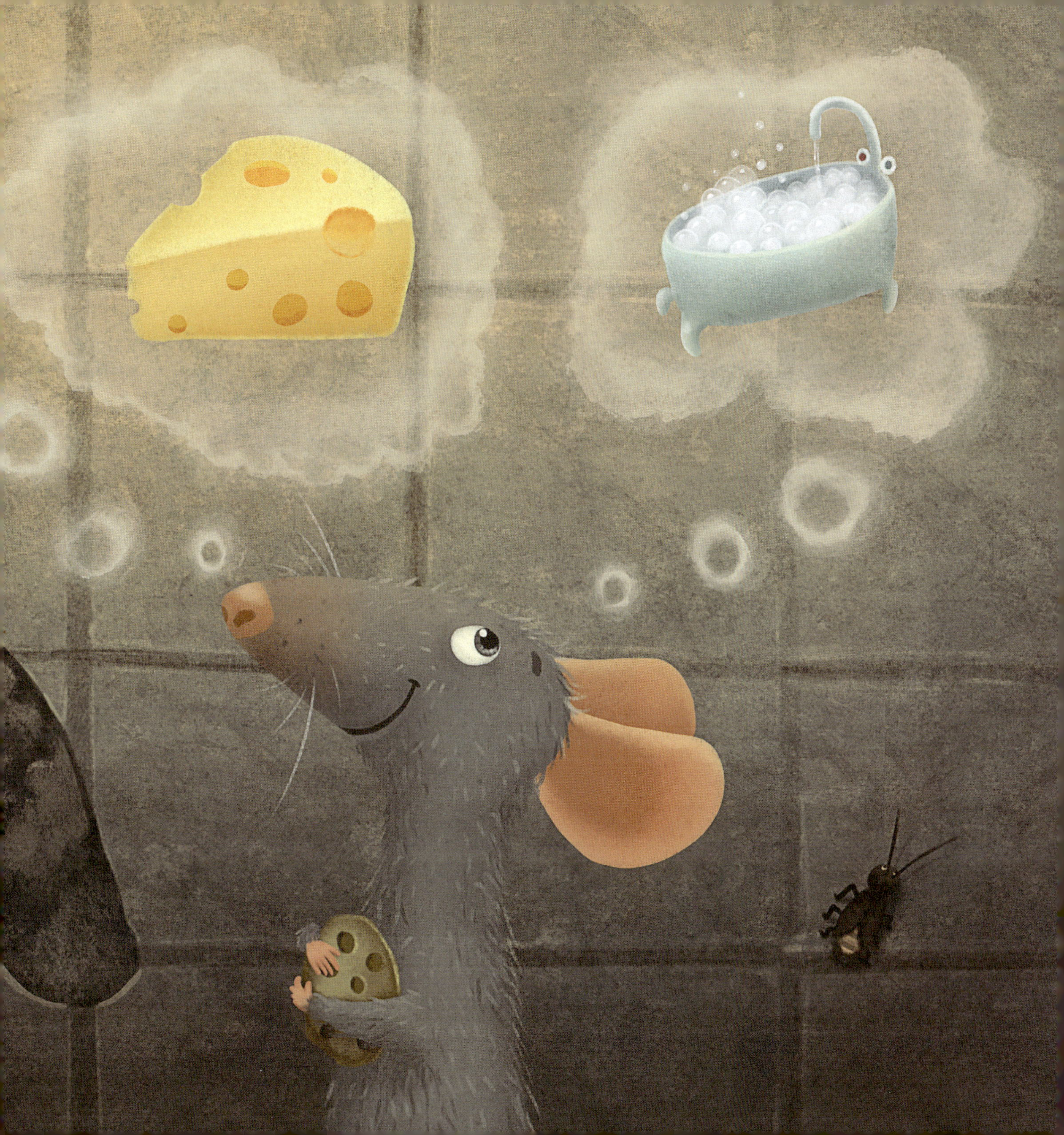

Small Elvin was thrilled. Oh, what a joy!
Soon, he would meet his beloved boy!
Smart Brayden showed him an underground map
and surely did know to avoid the trap.

As those two mice did wander around,
their ears heard nothing but a water sound.
Small Elvin was brave and learned to swim.
And hoped, like Brayden, to stay so slim.

They came to the rocks and had to jump
with one big pounce and then a bump!
The mice climbed fences and then back down.
They went across the great big town.

"Street life's not cozy as I always thought.
I miss my home and my life quite a lot!"
Then Elvin was happier than ever before
as he was in front of Connor's front door!

"Oh, Brayden! I just cannot thank you enough!"
The answer he heard in his ears was quite rough.
"Oh, please do not thank me but follow the deal!
I want a hot bath and a warm, juicy meal!"

Small Elvin brought bread with ham and cheese.
Poor Brayden had never tried any of these.
And then a hot bath and blossom soap.
And it was better than he could hope.

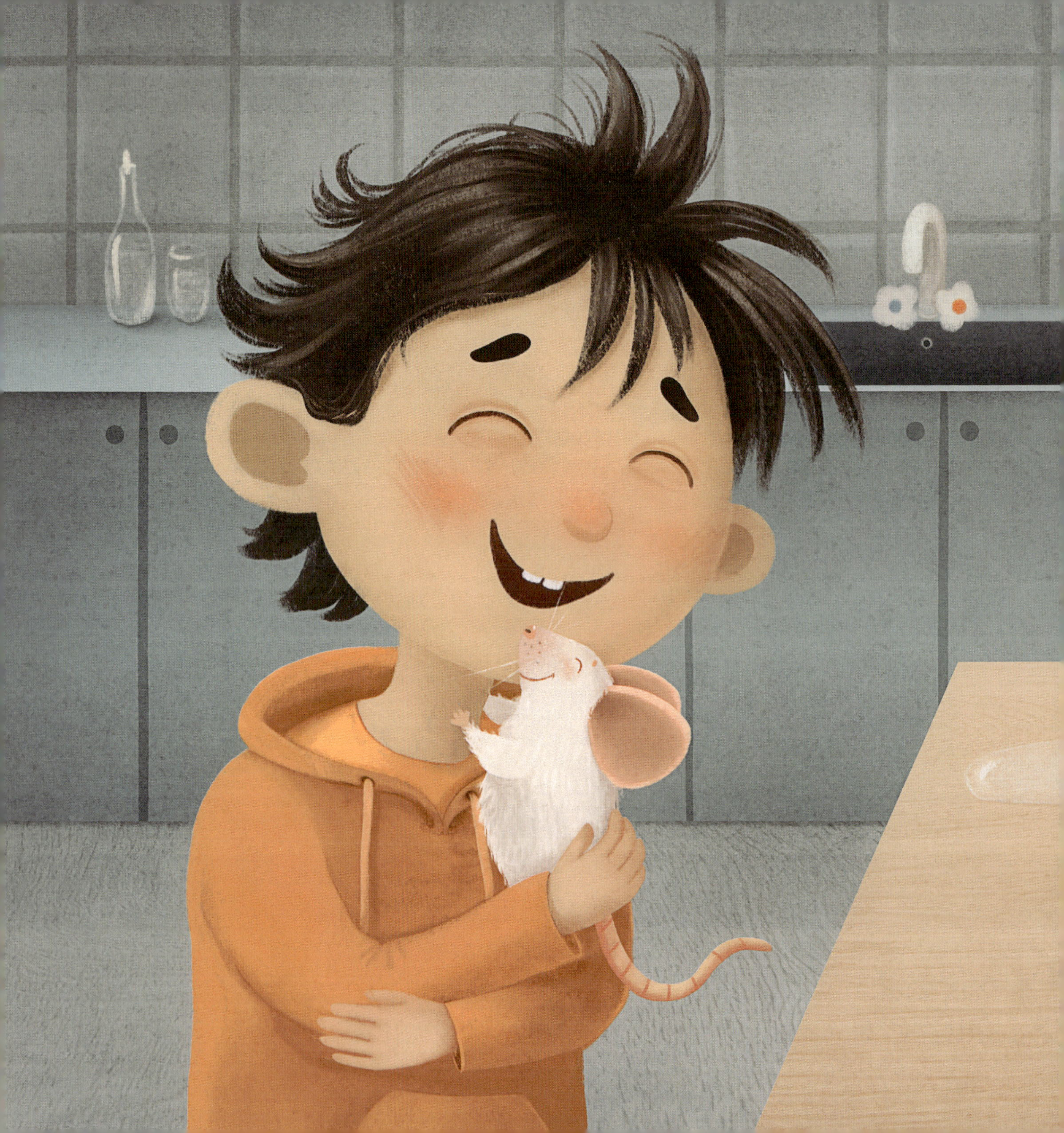

Then, clean and full, now ready to leave,
our Brayden then witnessed a beautiful scene.
Young Connor then opened and peeked through the door
and hugged our Elvin like never before!

"My Elvin! I thought I'd surely lost you!
I see that you have brought a friend, too!"
Those words would touch another's heart,
but Brayden planned to still depart.

Small Elvin was happy to see the boy and wanted now Brayden to feel that joy. "Oh, won't you stay and be my friend?" he asked, but Brayden did not intend.

"You love me today, and tomorrow I'll be out!
You will not trick this clever snout!
I know it well as I saw it before.
I do not believe in friends anymore!"

Then Elvin did cry, "No, that is not true!
See, I have a friend, which you can have too!
You might be happy, oh, can't you see?
Just open your heart, and you can trust me!"

Then Brayden stopped short to think for a while.
His look was more pleasant and less hostile.
"It would be nice to have a friend,"
that mouse decided in the end.

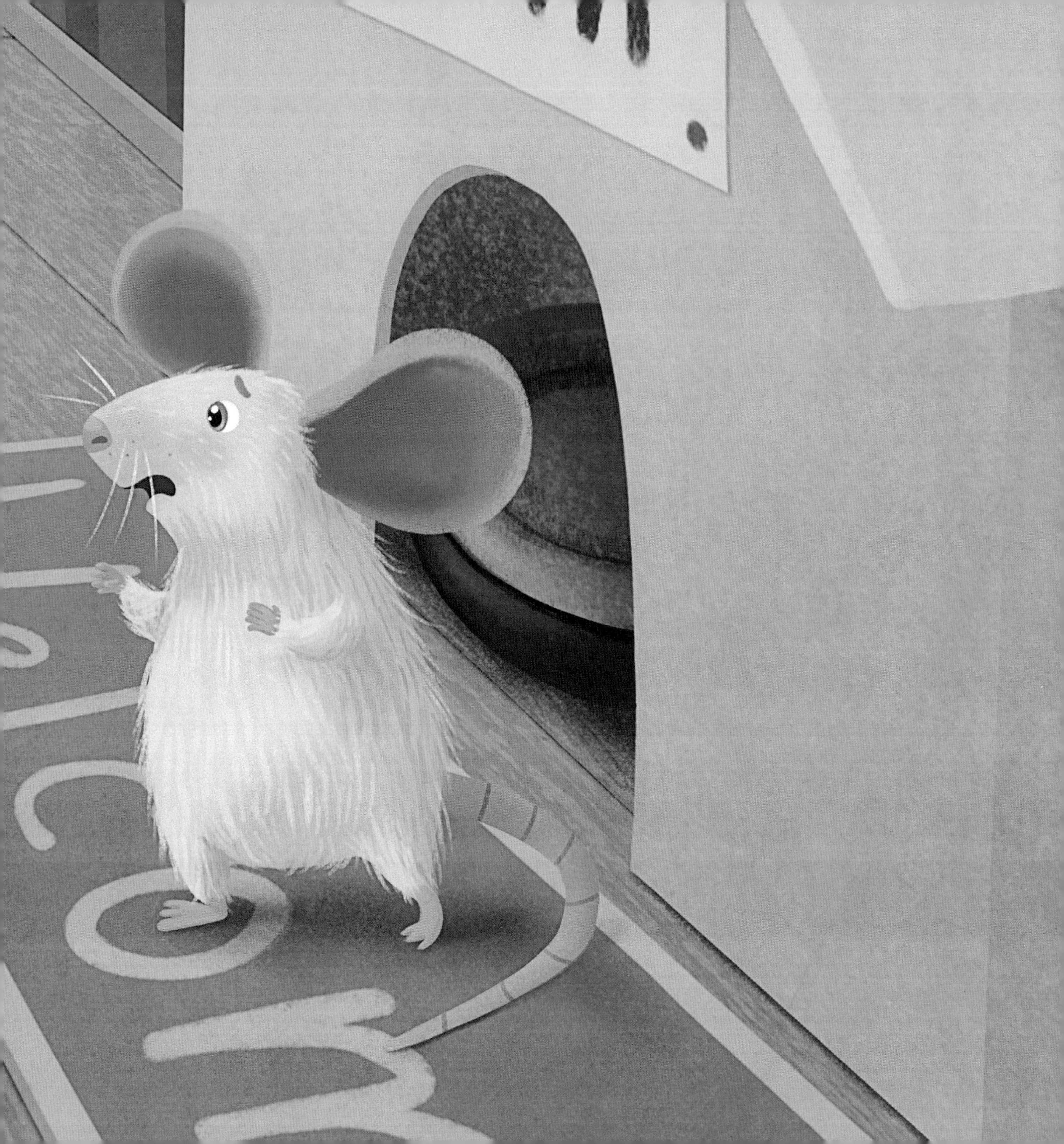

As Connor then smiled, Elvin did the same,
and Brayden felt love but also shame.
The shame for his heart, so cold and severe,
and love to his friends, so true and sincere.

So Brayden felt joy that now was for real.
No longer felt lonely as he used to feel.
He now had a family, his life's missing part.
And all that it took was to open his heart.

From the Author:

Friends are a very important part of our lives, just like our
family members. They share happy moments with us
and support us when we feel sad.

We all have different friends during our lives.
But there is usually one friend who holds a special place in our hearts.
Maybe you already know your special friend,
or possibly you are about to meet them.

You might come across some fake friends and feel disappointed,
as mouse Brayden felt in the story. But hang onto your hope.
One day, you will meet your "Elvin," and it will be
a true friendship for a lifetime.

Help Elvin find his way home

Dear reader,
Thank you so much for reading this book.

Have you enjoyed the adventures of our mice?
I would be so glad if you would tell me your opinion.
A minute of your time means a lot to me.

I have good news for you – there will be more books about our dear mice! Your review will help me create more adventures!

I have one more good news for you! An adorable bonus gift is waiting for you on the website! I'm sure you'll like it!

Well, that's all for now. I need to start writing the next book.
I look forward to your review.

Love,
Sandra

You can find your free gift by visiting my site

sandrajmorrison.com

or by scanning this QR-code

Printed in Great Britain
by Amazon